, said the shotgun to the head.

Also by Saul Williams

$S\sqrt{he}$

The Seventh Octave

, said the shotgun to the head.

Saul Williams

POCKET BOOKS

New York   London   Toronto   Sydney   Singapore

POCKET BOOKS, a division of Simon & Schuster, Inc.
1230 Avenue of the Americas, New York, NY 10020

Page vi: Paul Robeson, from *Paul Robeson Speaks,* Kensington Publishing Corporation. First published by Citadel Press/Carol Publishing/Carol Communications, Copyright 1978 Bruner Mazel, Inc. "The Night/1," from *The Book of Embraces* by Eduardo Galeano, translated by Cedric Belfrage with Mark Schafer. Copyright © 1989 by Eduardo Galeano. English translation copyright © 1991 by Cedric Belfrage. Used by permission of the author and W. W. Norton & Company, Inc.

Page 3: "All Those Ships That Never Sailed," from a poem by Bob Kaufman in *The Ancient Rain: Poems 1956-1978,* copyright 1958, New Directions Publishing Corporation.

ISBN: 0-7434-7079-6

First MTV Books/Pocket Books trade paperback edition September 2003

10 9 8 7 6 5 4 3 2 1

Art Direction: Jeffrey Keyton and Deklah Polansky
Design: Christopher Truch and Paul Raphaelson
Project Management: Sarah James

Manufactured in the United States of America

For information regarding special discounts for bulk purchases, please contact Simon & Schuster Special Sales at 1-800-456-6798 or business@simonandschuster.com.

To my mother

The man who accepts Western values absolutely, finds his creative faculties becoming so warped and stunted that he is almost completely dependent on external satisfactions, and the moment he becomes frustrated in his search for these, he begins to develop neurotic symptoms, to feel that life is not worth living, and, in chronic cases, to take his own life.

PAUL ROBESON

I can't sleep. There is a woman stuck between my eyelids. I would tell her to get out if I could. But there is a woman stuck in my throat.

EDUARDO GALEANO

INTRODUCTION

Have you ever been kissed by God? Passionately (tongue, lips, etc.)? Or are you one who simply condemns God to the realm of the invisible? When do you feel most comfortable? When do you feel most loved? Perhaps it is in the warm embrace of your lover or in the assuring touch of your mother. Perhaps, like me, you have likened this person to God in your life and realized that God was loving you through them. Or maybe you don't believe in God. Cool. Here's a simpler question: Have you ever lost yourself in a kiss? I mean pure psychedelic inebriation. Not just lustful petting but transcendental metamorphosis when you became aware that the greatness of this being was breathing into you. Licking the sides and corners of your mouth, like sealing a thousand fleshy envelopes filled with the essence of your passionate being and then opened by the same mouth and delivered back to you, over and over again—the first kiss of the rest of your life. A kiss that confirms that the universe is aligned, that the world's greatest resource is love, and maybe even that God is a woman. With or without a belief in God, all kisses are metaphors decipherable by allocations of time, circumstance, and understanding.

This book is the result of a kiss. A kiss that brings symbols to life and fear-based shortcomings to their symbolic death. To be kissed by a deity is nothing short of a miracle. The mind altering/altaring effects can last more than a lifetime. Here is the account of a man so ravished by a kiss that it distorts his highest and lowest frequencies of understanding into an incongruent mean of babble and brilliance. He wanders the streets disheveled and tormented by all that he sees that does not reflect her love. He is a wandering man, sort of like a modern day John the Baptist, telling of the coming of a female messiah that he has known intimately. He is the babbling man you cross the street to avoid. He is the unavoidable end before the new beginning. He is a lover in search of greater love. SHE is One and many: Kali, the Hindu goddess of destruction and creation; Oya, the Yoruba orisha of death and rebirth; the Holy Ghost, which is to say, the woman restored to her rightful place in the Holy Trinity. No longer ghost, no longer virgin, SHE is mother of us all.

saul williams,
Los Angeles, 2003

CITIZENS,

children of the night,
bearers of the day torch:
scorched and burned.

BURN NOT.

the dam is broken.
the curse is fled.
once muddied and still,
the river runs

RED!

"ALL

those ships that never sailed
the ones with their seacocks open
that were scuttled in their stalls

TODAY

i bring them back

HUGE AND INTRANSITORY

and let them sail

FOREVER!"*

if ever
there were currents
uncurrent

the wind
could not serve as
truth's currency

CURRENTLY

MOON MARKED

AND

SUN SPARKED

UNMARKED BILLS

W~~ILL~~ i AM

CERTAIN

i SPEAK A NEW LANGUAGE

as is **ALWAYS**

THE FIRST SIGN

of a

NEW AGE

i had begun to believe my blackened toenails
were on path to decay when, in truth,
they had begun the gradual process of

CRYSTALLIZATION.

i am he who walks on wind scorned feet with toenails of

AMETHYST AND ROSE QUARTZ.

my path now crystal clear.

i AM COME TO TELL YOU

SHE IS HERE.

it is not written

NO pen *MAN* ship

was ever **CARGOED**

with her character

NOTE:

BOOKS ARE CAREFULLY FOLDED FORESTS

void of autumn

BOUND FROM THE

SUN

Likewise, she made her residence

ON THE OUTSKIRTS
OF A SHADOWING HISTORY
ON THE DARKSIDE OF THE MOON

where the searchlight of the sun

COULD NOT SPOT HER
nor rot her
the seed of forbidden fruit
every tree
HAS A HIDDEN ROOT

YET, SHE HAS
COME TO LIGHT

THE SWELLING PATCHWORK
OF VIBRANT DREAMS

YES, THERE IS A SCIENCE
TO THE AROMA
OF SLEEPING WOMEN

(AND TO THINK OF THE GIRLFRIEND i WAS TEMPTED TO BREAK UP WITH BECAUSE SHE SLEPT TOO MUCH) i now know, they *NURTURED* her there:

they slept in packs

dreamt in cycles

NURSED HER IN SHIFTS

and **became** her

ON ROTATION

unnamed her

everytime she was named
so she would not be known to anyone

(even unto herself)

undressed her

everytime she was dressed

so she would not be recognized

as anyone other than herself

they blindfolded her

and spun her
in circles

so she would

find her way here

by no other means

than her **intuition**

and
she
is
come

i am a simple disoriented man
in her presence

i wear my loincloth

over my eyes

and ejaculate

too soon

forgive me father
for i have sinned

i prayed to you
and cupped

the wind

and in doing so

barred her entry

into a century:

100 years
of solitude

(yes, the wind is the moon's imagination wandering)

i will now pray
with my hands

outstretched
with these psalms

etched
into my palms

most beloved,

i am certain of nothing more

than your **existence**

a thousand ants

crawling under a log

may find themselves exposed

in my childlike search

for you

i have spent lifetimes
in monasteries
and drum stretched
villages
in expectation

of this:

our

ecstatic dance

my kali flower
i am eternally destroyed
by your love

no longer

am i eligible

for any worker's

pension

my friends laugh at me
and talk behind my back

they say that you have

changed me

and

i am

i am like a survivor

of the flood

walking through the streets

drenched with

God

surprised that all of the

drowned victims

are still walking and talking

maybe there's **hope**

i rush to each victim's side
sucking what i can of you
out of your various

incarnations

pumping their stomachs

and filling them

to touch them

is to touch you

to kiss them

is to kiss you

my friends,

love is an *artform*
slightly removed
from its element

one may ask

well what does this mean?

i respond

i've made it up
but it shall be

from now on

from now on

cities

will be built

on **one** side

of the street

so that soothsayers
will have wilderness to wander

and lovers

space enough

to contemplate

a kiss

she kissed

as if she, **alone,**

could forge

the signature

of the sun

i closed my eyes

although
i never knew
the difference
i stood before
a brighter light
at lesser
distance

and then, a feeling. Almost as if nothing were ever bound to repeat itself again. As if history had been as masterfully created as the great pyramids and any attempt to reconstruct or relive any given moment would have to stem from an understanding of how the pyramids were built from the

top down.

and if one could understand such majesty one
would also understand that **kisses** hold codes
for unlocking new portals and that **pyramids**
were first made of **flesh**

                                        our bonded souls
                                        shifting through
                                          hidden corrals
                                      and passageways
i will find my way
to eternity
within you

when i can feel you
breathing into me
i, like a stone gargoyle
atop some crumbling building,
spring to life
a resuscitated
angel

i sweep through city streets
my wings out-stretched
making mothers
clutch their young
and remember

and do you remember, dear ones
or has your history forsaken you?
there were tales told 'round fires
mysteries coded in song
chants and uprisings
centuries of art

all incantations
calling forth this day

on this day

the drunks vomit in unison

'though last night they drank from different cups

children laugh and play

introducing their parents

to invisible friends

a country girl smiles

and two trees blossom

out of season

sea sons awaken
our mother has returned
to wave us
from uncertainty
once **tidal**

twice born
of **wooden ships**
thrice formed
through mother's hips
mother ships
graced **tu lips**
a poet's garden

"2 for 5"
"they're going fast"
the future's bargain
"that's strange"
"i heard my name"
the river's parting
"hurry up"
things blurry up
the sun is darkened

rivers
like oceans
oceans
like answers
questions
in cloud forms
raindrops
in stanzas

to be
or not to...

to see
or not to...

she had eyes
like two turntables
mix(h)**er**

in between

my dreams   **and reality**
blend in
ancient themes

the bass is of isis

(basis)

cross-faded to **ankh**

the beat drops

like a cliff

over-looking

my heart

6000 feet
above
sea level

3300 bodies
disassembled

the head bone's
connected
to the cock pit

knee jerk
ass backwards

dancing slaves
in a mosh pit

punk rock
of gibraltar
roll out
nothing's new

mo' blood dyes
the mo hawk
only this time
it's you

and you
never loved her
for what she
possessed

you powdered
her face
and came
on her
head-dress

47

oil slicked feathers, putrid stenched water-bed
"mother nature's a whore," said the shotgun to the head.

and it smelled like teen spirit

angst driven insecure

a country in puberty

a country at war

wet dreams

cotton mouth

blood thirsty

oily hair

fast cars

movie stars

earn 20 mill...

to instill fear

she and i never spoke. we were in relationships we shouldn't have been in. we were sorcerers who had stored their charms in unmarked boxes because they had made our partners uncomfortable. every day, we reported to work early in order to rest our waking eyes on last nights dream. i had resorted to sleeping with my back to my partner. the ball i slept curled in became the question mark i now placed within all prior commitments. this was no teenage crush. it was an adulthood rite. she was what love had grown up to be: unspoken, yet shared between us.

on that glorious day, i stood before my cubicle shuffling papers like a card reader with an oversized deck. the one on top read, "invoice", as something within told me to turn around. she walked the aisle towards me perhaps on the same undisclosed mission that now leads me towards her, only neither of us was confident enough to slow our pace as we approached the other. we brushed shoulders moments before the first explosion. we, both, stopped, turned back and stared at each other as if shocked that the outside world might bring to life our inner workings.

here is our first touch

and here is this trembling building

hold the two in your hands

and tell me what you come up with

everyone running to windows to see what has happened, as smiles slowly rise on our faces like the time between 6:24 and 6:39 over the skyline. we are not panicked, only awed at how a fluttering stomach can predict the short life span of a social butterfly. love has become a fiery place. but we are living in an old testament where there is a faith that does not burn, that turns kings into believers.

i believe that those were my exact thoughts before extending my hand, just as she did hers. and as we walked into the grasp of the other, a second explosion. we smiled, knowingly, like scientists witnessing the primordial origins of chemistry. and down that burning aisle where glass had been strewn like rice we decided to jump the broom, walking off into the will of the divine wind {<**jap. equiv. to kami=divine + kaze=wind**} .

she held my hand
leaving three fingers
in my grasp

like gripping a symbol
from the i ching
which i'm not sure
i've ever grasped

o my friends,

the greatest americans

have not been born yet

they are waiting patiently

for the past

to die

please
give
blood

those crumbled tablets
were to share a story
with a burning Bush

where is that voice from nowhere
to remind us
that the holy ground
we walk on
purified by native blood
has rooted trees
whose fallen leaves
now color code
a sacred list of demands?

who among us can give translation
of autumn hues to morning news?

the anchor man
thrown overboard
has simply rooted us
in history's repeating cycle

a nation in its *saturn years*

that won't acknowledge *karma*

where is that voice from nowhere?

the one your prophets spoke of?

there are voices from **fear**
disconnected from their diaphragms
dangling from coffee covered teeth
that spill into our laps
and burn our privates

there are voices
from the sides of necks
some already noosed
dangling participles
pronouns running
for sentence
serving life
in corner offices
and ghetto corners
their voices are the same:
dead to themselves
numb to the possibility
of truth existing beyond
that which they can palm
in the bleeding hole
of their hands,
period.

there are voices of elders
who seem to do no more
than damn us
to our childish ways

for in many households

wisdom
no longer comes with age

so where is that voice from nowhere?
that burning bush?
that passing dove?

I hear voices of generals calling for ammunition

voices of presidents
calling for arms

voices of women
calling for help

but where is that voice from nowhere?

that God of abraham?
those crying rocks?

can he be heard over the gunfire

the whizz of passing missles

the crash of buildings

the cries of children

the crack of bones

the shriek of sirens?

or is that his mighty voice?

your angry god

craving the sacrifice

of a virgin generation's

son degenerate

your holy books: written in red ink on burning sands

(...branded into necks, whipped into backs, forced inside of vaginas and anuses, crammed into mouths, rubbed into open sores...)

your prayers
between rounds
do no more
than fasten the fate
of your children
to the hammered truth
of your trigger

a truth that mushrooms
its darkened cloud
over the rest of us
so that we too
bear witness
to the short-lived fate
of a civilization
that worships

a male god

your weapons

are phallic

all of them

the dummy
that sits on your lap
is no longer
a worthwhile spectacle
his shrunken pale face
leaves little room
for imagination
we have spotted
your moving lips
and have pinned the voice
to its proper source

it is a source of madness

a source of hunger for power

a source of weakness

we are exiting your colosseum
and encircling your box office
demanding our families back
our rituals back
our cultures back
our language back
and our gods
so that we may return them
to their proper source
the source of life
the source of creation

the womb of the **Great Mother**
we will cut through
the barbed wire hangers and chastity belts

we will climb in
and incubate our spirits
through the winter

we will wait through the degenerate course
of your repeated ~~history~~
we will wait for the past to die

pools of blood
are not recreational

even lifeguards drown
when the undertow breaks bread with the under belly

demons disguised as sharks

have not put enough thought into their costumes

a wiseman stays ashore

when pointed fins

read like italian subtitles

the end is near (...)
the beginning

in the beginning her tears were the long awaited rains of a parched somali village. red dusted children danced shadows in the new found mounds of mascara that eclipsed her face, reflected in the smogged glass of carlos' east street bodega. learning to love, SHE had forgotten to cry. seldom hearing the distant thunder in her lover's ambivalent sighs. HE was not honest. SHE was not sure. a great grandfather had sacrificed the family's clarity for gold in the late eighteen hundreds. nonetheless, SHE had allowed him to mispronounce her name, which had eventually led to her misinterpreting her own

dreams. and, later, doubting them.
but the night was young....

...as a child, she played for hours with children never bothering to
learn their names. they forged

friendships and charters to nations that still
stand.

she is president
of a sliding board

her citizens surrender to the exuberance of
falling

knowing they **will land**
on their feet

...her uncle would swallow pictures of God
to be sure that God was inside of him

they institutionalized his stomach lining
'til he choked on his own belief system

the truth was in his vomit
she is within us

cut to

a world of dreams
fluid and unremembered
a multitude of tongues
universed
women adorned
bracelets beaded
with possible conclusions
to stories
that will never end

our maned character sits in a long dark brown leather chair that is contoured to fit his entire body (an antique chair, perhaps, from one of old china's opium dens). in his lap is a book made of blue and brown strips of fabric. definitely handmade. the pages are yellow, grainy and uneven. as if each page were torn to fit as opposed to cut. the book is bound by thin hemp strings. from over his right shoulder, we read as he writes:

i PRAYED
AND THEN i THREW UP

it WAS WEIRD bECAUSE i'VE bEEN WANTING to THROW UP
i'VE bEEN FEELING THE NEED to
A NEED i'VE NEVER FELT bEFORE

i THREW UP
A yellow bile
EXActly AFTER
THE MOST ECSTATIC MOMENT OF pRAYER
i HAVE EVER EXPERIENCED

A PRAYER THAT i KNEW
WAS bEING FULFILLED
AS i SPOKE it

i AM ONLY RESPONSIbLE to MY DREAMS
THE FULFILLMENT OF DREAMS

i KNOW WHAT it MEANS to SAY "GOD IS ON MY SIDE". EVEN NOW,
WHEN i FEEL likE THERE IS SO MUCH RED tApE bETWEEN MY
DREAMS AND THE REST OF THE WORLD. i REMEMbER, AS A littLE
boy, cUTTING THAT RED tApE FOR MY GODFATHERS NEW
bUILDING. yES, RED tApE IS OFTEN cUT IN CEREMONIES bEFORE
DOORS ARE OPENED.

he looks up from his book and spots a shadow approaching his door.
he writes:

AND NOW tHE journalist HAS ARRIVED

he drops his pen and then picks it up and quickly scribbles, as we
hear a soft knock on the door:

but not before
i DROP MY PEN
IN tHE SAME place
i vomited

Journalist: What are you working on?

Maned Character: An attack of the subconscious.

J: Why?

MC: Because it's eating us alive.

J: How would you characterize the subconscious of America, in particular, the youth of America?

MC: As characterized. We are acting out the parts of age old scripts.

J: Is there any way past that?

MC: No.

J: Then wouldn't that render your work useless?

MC: No.

J: Why not?

MC: There's always room for improvisation.

J: You mean, then, that we cannot help but act out our parts because "it is written," but we can still find space to riff on what isn't written.

MC: Exactly. This is an appeal to the unwritten histories of the future.

J: Aren't you, then, doing the universe or humanity or the future some sort of disservice by writing it down.

MC: Not really. Even with literacy rates going up, people don't read as much as they did in the past, or rather the written word doesn't carry as much weight. Or, at least, newly written words don't. We're still living out an old testament. What i'm doing is sort of a *lyrical* hacking. i'm figuring a way to fool the database into thinking that this book is older than it is. i've sampled elements of the code and dated aspects of the language. Sort of like post dating a check, but in reverse. Thus, the signals and symbols being sent to the database are old yet they register in a different way. And when the individual reading a passage decides to quit and then is asked by the database whether or not they would like to save the changes made to the document, i am hoping that they will mechanically click "yes".

J: And what if people don't read it?

MC: It will already be bound.

J: Bound?

MC: Yes, a book is always bound. And written word is often bound...to happen. It increases its likelihood. But really, as long as MTV markets it right, it should reach a lot of people. It's carefully designed for the short attention span.

J: Would you characterize yourself as different?

MC: Well, it's also written this way because my attention span is pretty short.

behold, a story untold

I HAVE SEEN THE MOON
IN A SUN DRESS

the ocean
beneath her
rippling in laughter
at the sight
of a lone man
who learned to walk on water
for a glimpse
of his truth
in her crater

i have found the library
where all the dreams deferred
were stored

catalogues of cultures
indexed by communal disappearance

mayans are metaphors
for astral doors
left cracked
by children afraid
to sleep in utter darkness

i am unafraid to utter
darkness
i speak a shadowed truth
like a **newborn**
wrapped in a blanket
tucked tight enough
to resemble

its mother's celestial cave

i am handing this child
to you
the godparent
of a foreshadowing
soon to be revealed
**when you remove
the plastic seal**

come see
how death is a myth

there are no deceased
only deceived
death only awaits
those who believed

i surrendered
my beliefs
and found myself
at the tree of life
injecting my story
into the veins
of leaves
only to find that stories
like forests
are subject to seasons

i am the deads latest experiment
a midwife birthing afterlife

the unborn are fully present
we have disguised ourselves
from ourselves
so that our daily thoughts
may not sabotage
our spirits'
ascendance

thrice immersed
into the wordly
we are
self-forgotten

for our own benefit

i am forced
to disassemble
my being
to fit into your monitor

i hand you my spirit
as i walk through
customs

i am to be reassembled
after the final check point

sorcery of self:
a phrase i coined
and now surrender to you

it's as if i've swallowed
an interior decorator

i like my heart where it is

i cannot make
your past disappear

only rabbits, my love,
only rabbits

depleted memory banks
have grounded our emotional economy

.

**we have been forced
to create a new currency**

one that will truly allow us
to love our neighbors
for reasons beyond guilt and pity

i have offered myself
to the inkwell of the wordsmith
that i might be shaped
into new terms of being

only through new words
might new worlds
be called
into order

i stretch my body
into your symbols of statehood

i am a citizen
casting my vote
and net
in the same breath

i dare not keep what i reap
i am only fishing
for momentary companionship

i have committed myself
to adultery
i will only sleep
with GOD's wife

our affair
is no secret
he gets his thrills
from watching us

i cannot tear myself
from her eyes
i am, indeed,
her pupil
and no longer fear
the unseen

teach me thy ways o lord

steady my hands
upon your breasts
and guide me
to your altar

swallow me whole

so that i may
be born
again

a great one has said
that poets are midwives
to reality

yet these words
catch me
when i would have them
let me go

✝omb

that cross
did nothing more
than make a death chamber
of a nursery

i became
as a child
only after

i had entered
the kingdom

introduce me
to your after-life
let me see
if i can tempt it
from its cloud form

those white robes
are the very cloaks
of your enemies
and their leader
has the brazen tone
of your shepherd

maybe you shouldn't have prayed
with your eyes closed

open eyes plainly see
the resemblance

a prayer stamped

return to sender

tables over turned

in a temple

bitten apples
that encourage you
to think different

God has hair
on her pussy
and waits
burning with desire
for you

this is no blasphemy
you have erected
ancient penises
in your capitols
and prayed
in the name
of a father
a male child
and a ghost

i am only revealing
what was hidden
under the floating
white sheet

the same sheet
you crawled under
to reach ecstasy
with your lover

the same sheet
under which
you created life
and progeny

unfasten your mind
from your fears

you cower behind your God
as he leads you into slavery
and war

your curren(cy)t-sea

reflects an army
of dead men

the moon is ignored

you, too, can become
her cyclical sacrament

your children drown
in the cross-fire

you throw search parties
for a profit (f=ph)
and pray
to your rev.enue

your dead ancestors
re-die
in air tight vaults

they conspire
to seduce your children

you have done nothing
to protect them
from the evil eye

i serve
a living God

she is a distorted horn solo
fingered by the hand
of a master

time's signature
has done no more
than punctuate
her curvature

God plays a human instrument

wind pipes horny
when tongue kisses reed
heart beats bump
over-turned tables

heads nod in affirmation

yes, yes, y'all
you don't stop

not even when every sign
tells you that you should

your father's diet
kills him
and you hire
his chef

you wage war
on minimum wage
and the people
purchase their delicacies
from Target

maybe you should aim
elsewhere

a prince
sings of thieves
in a temple

you call your doctor
complaining
of a migraine

she loads
2 leaden pills
into a 3 pound needle
and asks you
where it hurts

hers is the song
you cannot get
from your head

you blame your thoughts
on magdalene
and let bostonians
wash your feet

your sidewalks
scuff your wingtips

your angels fly
through barrels

monkeys laugh at them

intelligence is intuitive
you needn't learn to love
unless you've been taught
to fear and hate

your students
kill each other
and their teachers

they are angry
at not being taught
that pink and floyd
were blues singers
quarantined
from the source of power
that would project their image
as well as their sound

and those
who do not know
their history
are bound to repeat it

unbound, she made her residence
on the dark side of the moon

she detangled herself
from her bed-post
and washed
your crusted fears away

**"massa always do dat
when miss betsy done gone
to visit her sista. he cain't wait
to tie dat poor sarah up and
have his way wid her"**

your ancestors smile up
from your backpockets

you buy another candy bar

your teeth rot

your head still aches

you've gotta do something
about this migraine

your analyst works overtime

your broker calls
urging you to sell your stock
in a certain prescription drug company
before tomorrow's news
hits the stands

your life savings
in dead men's currency

you keep your gun
in your desk drawer

movies have taught you
your hiding places

silver screens with bare walls
behind them

the illustrators of bare walls
projected their dreams
beyond their fears

theirs were the walls
of pyramids

yours are the walls
of crumbled towers

the truth still stands

alone
at the dance
waiting for you
to take her hand

you only need ask

you sit behind your desk
ready to aim
at the cloaked thief
in your temple

the spooked groom
who mistakes his bride
for a ghost

she can no longer hide
her form behind her veil

you are a cocked trigger
smuggled into a house of prayer

the statues arouse
your blood to wine

her essence
cupped in her being
she has made herself
available to you

she needn't steal your heart
if you give it to her

the cops and robbers
of your childhood
neglected to teach you
such simplicity

i came to know her
before she overthrew
my government

it was no conspiracy
only an unraveling
of a fist

her charm
is in her silence
she speaks
in extended parenthesis

hers is the voice from nowhere

the earth
her diaphragm
she speaks
through wind
always giving reverence
to her molten core

fathered by sun and sky
we are offspring of spring
reborn from the bounty
of her nourishment

our father gives
in the one way he knows
she makes the dough
and bids him bake
our daily bread

we set our table at twilight
and hold hands
offering grace to the wind
acknowledging that even he who shines
was born out of the mystery
of her darkness

our mother holds no judgment
she absorbs our father's light
into her flesh and blood
regenerating
an offering universal

God is a single mother

to the eldest of her children
she is known by many names
they build their fires
in the night
and tune into her windsong
each dance is known by heart
and foot and mouth

the frenzy of the fire
is our own unquenched desire
to become the one
she takes into her house

have you ever been?
are you experienced?
have you ever been
to electric lady land?
did you drink from the fountain?
did you bask in her molten core?
did she call your name
and guide you to her peak?
did you feel her quake and tremble?
did you feel the need to restrain her?
did she unmask her loving fury?
did she frighten you?
did you question what it felt like
to have someone inside of you?
to swallow life and incubate
a world to come?
did you ask her how it felt
to be God incarnate?
to be daughter of the moon
bearing the sun?

this is her body

this is her blood

tithes and offerings
made to the father
have kept buddha laughing
he knows that dharmic needs
are karmic deeds undone

a love supreme
summoned from dreams
fuses now
with the hereafter
as spirit to flesh
is melded by the sun

oya, kali ma
here is an offering
these words recited
from my heart
to yours and yours

i am thankful for the trees
shaped into coffins
that we now shred
to bed these words
within our cores

paper mills
may you recycle
all that was stolen
and/or lost
so that these newest testaments
might come at lesser costs

what is the cost of freedom?
and how is it paid?

to be free
of the rigmarole
of age old traditions
based on submission and fear
one must pay with the courage
to stand alone

to be free
of the restraints
of a culture
that instills the will
of material possession and domination
into its citizens
one must learn to honor
the substance of their materials
and the etymological roots
of their findings

mater: fr. Latin.meaning mother

this *is* a material world

your priests and presidents
no longer matter

only you and i, my love

in order to commune
we must dismiss the false gods
we have granted domain
over our will and testament

this earth is our sanctuary
nothing more need be built

our mother
has erected
mountains of quartz
we only need climb
to synchronize our hearts
with hers

the truth
erupts from her core

we court a corrupted institution
subject to the division of its faculty

we are tenured students of intuition

professors of a truth beyond reason
schooled in the over priced cities
in the valleys of our consciousness

we are charged
for our own discharge

we look to the mother
knowing that our imposed tuition
will be covered

install our payment plans
in pele's tears

all disaster
is both natural
and preventable
but imposed force
will only manifest
your fears

come, my love
we have mountains to climb
wilderness to wander

you have shown me
a love that cannot be
given or taken

let us bask
in the fullness
of ourselves

a simple kiss
now blood and breath
both awakened

a balanced diet
to sustain
life and health

we will wax and wane
in attention given from our father
we can trust he will return
yet, she is here

she has granted us this land
to forge her cycle
and when we doubt
places the ocean
in our tears

come, my love
we have oceans to sail

the painted nature
of this earth
is water-based
and will fade
if not tended

let us retrace the origin
of a kiss

they have ravished
your heart and mind
but your breath
travels freely
out of your mouth
and into mine

there is the current
i wish to sail

here is a love
uncharted

throw away your map
and swallow
this cratered pill

pull it from the sky
and let it dissolve
under your tongue

it is only a matter of time
before we are timeless

do you feel it yet?

wow

i can trace
each shadow
back to its origin

can you feel it yet?

drink more water
take deeper breaths

wow

why have i been
so afraid of love?
so afraid of being vulnerable?
so afraid of being open?

it's like
every mannerism and gesture
was a lie
some sort of shield
to protect me
from the judgment
of others

oh my god
turn the music up

wow

do you feel that bass line?

it feels like a snake

how could you not
yield to temptation?

why would you not?

dance!

yeah!

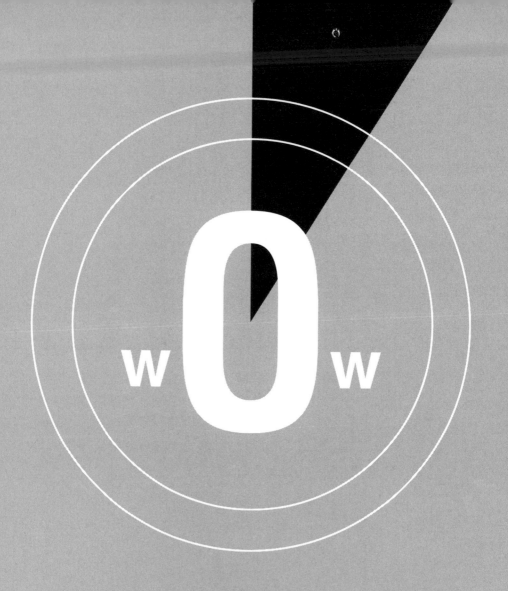

eve was just open

and that's what scared

that father/sun god

ha! that's why they named her eve

they were just afraid of the dark

scared of their mother's own womb

afraid of the unknown

what happens to a society
when mystery is labeled
as evil?

it yields an ever-connected chain
of false labels and misinterpretations

the indigenous are labeled
as savage terrorists
and plotted against

the open-hearted
are manipulated into slavery

the vulnerable are penetrated
by force of law

citizens
where is your allegiance?

why do you pledge
with a covered heart
when it needs be opened?

why do you bear arms
with balled fists
and closed palms?

why do you call yourself
a patriot (pater: fr. Latin.meaning father)
when your greatest love has always been
for your mother?

this loaded phallus
has becum
the prevailing metaphor
of the day

you've spent your chi
on cheap versions
of the virgin

you've worshipped
loopholes in a story
and war shipped
mythic men to glory

if in god's image
then your god's
a plastic surgeon

a tyrannic dictator

a coward behind a curtain
with a megaphone

an aging oil tycoon
on viagra
ramming his plow
into the earth
turning up disease
and disaster
out of an ever-drying womb

you will become her cyclical sacrament

menstrual minstrels
footing your own bill
of right left right
marching blindly
into a moonless night
another dimension
where children use chalk
on the sidewalk
tracing their bodies
for the precriminal investigation
of their paternal inheritance:

murder!

men in uniform
take note

love refuses
to take cover

the cloaked enchantress
of your faith
now prevails

if you refuse

yourself and her

then take the fire

from your holster

and **lend your breath**

so that my love and i

may sail

ready

aim

fire!

water

earth

wind

ACKNOWLEDGMENTS

I am eternally indebted to so many who have helped bring this book to your hands: my literary agent, Charlotte Gusay, who works hard at keeping me from being a flake. Thank you everyone at MTV/Pocket Books for your commitment and for investing your talents and time into mine: Liate Stehlik at Pocket Books and Demond Jarrett, my editor. Jacob Hoye at MTV Books and all of the graphic designers and associates who have worked on this project. I would especially like to thank my manager, Sara Newkirk, and her assistant, Amirah, who have helped me envision a practical means of artistic growth and merit, and my lawyer, Jennifer Justice. I would like to offer all of you my sincere gratitude for being in your position and having the heart and savvy to honor mine. I pray that we all continue to work together to bring about the necessary fulfillment of our destinies.

Then I would like to thank the inspired spirit of beat poet Bob Kaufman. His legendary ten-year Buddhist vow of silence that began with the assassination of John F. Kennedy in 1963 and ended ten years later when he decreed, "All those ships that never sailed . . . ," has resonated very deeply within me. There is, perhaps, no greater discipline than that of a channeling poet who chooses to remain silent. His silence was in response to death and assassination and, thus, I must also thank those who have died and those who have killed for playing their role in the unfolding of the present. Their many spirits are cargoed in this pen/man/ship.

I would also like to thank Allen Ginsberg, who kissed me three weeks before his death and told me of the power of chanting OM. His voice, along with the voice of Imamu Amiri Baraka, echoed through my mind as I wrote this poem. So, to all of the poets of the Beat Generation and the Black Arts/Power Movement, thank you for your voices and canon.

Another great inspiration was the Persian Sufi poet Hafiz, whose commitment to God and poetry was beautifully blasphemous. His work is a gift to us all. Thus, I also extend my thanks to the translators who have made works such as his and Rumi's understandable to me.

Then I would like to thank all of my closest loved ones and friends simply for being my closest loved ones and friends (if you're someone who knows that I am actually very silly and not at all as serious as one might think, I am talking to you). I am thankful for all of the different realities that you have all brought into my life. Some of us don't talk as much as we used to, but I still look forward to that big commune where we can all get together and laugh and dance and tell all the wonderful stories of how we got from there to here and what we learned on the way.

And I would like to thank you, the reader, and whoever or whatever directed your attention to this book. Thank you for allowing these words into your mind and possibly your heart. Thank you for every kind word or thought. Thank you for the patience that it took to figure out what the fuck I was talking about on page X. Thank you for the discussions you may have and the people you may open. To inspire means to breathe in, to inhale. We are of common breath and purpose. I am inspired by your existence. There are many deities crowded into your flesh trying to get a glimpse of this world through your eyes. Upon meeting some of you I have felt them crowd into my being, sometimes elbowing and jabbing each other for a momentary glimpse of you through mine. I see your beauty and reflect it. I honor the GOD in you and pray that your prayers be answered in kisses.

May these words bring worlds,
saul williams